Out Of The Candy Jar

story and illustrations by
Merrijo Wheaton

For George,
Who inspires me every day.

PALMETTO
PUBLISHING

Charleston, SC
www.PalmettoPublishing.com

Out of the Candy Jar
Copyright © 2020 by Merrijo Wheaton

Hardcover ISBN: 978-1-64990-434-8
Paperback ISBN: 978-1-64990-567-3

If you found yourself in a forest some dark night, a place you had never been before, you might have happened upon the cottage of a most extraordinary wizard, Horace Windemere. You just might have smelled, and you probably would have, the wondrous concoctions that Horace creates in his magical kitchen.

Horace Windemere Wizard loved making candy and treats. He loved the way the kitchen smelled. He loved adding ingredients one by one. He loved the looks on children's faces as each sweet was enjoyed.

But more than anything, Horace loved creating new and unique treats. Treats like whirling toffee twinkles and chocolate candy poppers.

Horace always made
his candy at night,
for that is when magic
is most powerful.

Every evening yummy treats piled up
in Horace Windemere's kitchen.

Until -- the day Horace ran out of ideas
for new treats.

No matter how hard he thought, and he thought
quite a lot, nothing wonderful came to his mind.

Horace Windemere sat in his favorite thinking chair.   Surely an idea would come to him there, he thought.

But after a time of muddling and befuddling about the problem, Horace found himself exactly where he had started.
NO   NEW   IDEAS!

Horace simply did not want to make the kind of creations he had made before. He wanted something new and different.

Perhaps if he tried on a new hat.

That might help his thinking.

Or perhaps if he jumped up and down
on his bed 6 times
an idea would shake loose.

But still no new ideas came.
Horace was left with only a headache.

The shelves, usually stocked with magical treats, now were empty and sad. One little jelly bean sat all alone.

"This will never do," Horace muttered to himself as he stared at the lonely jelly bean.

But, as nothing came to mind, Horace just shuffled off to bed. There would be no fresh sweets waiting for children in the morning.

But something wonderful was happening that night in Horace Windemere's kitchen. Something he knew nothing about.

out of
treats

Now, Horace had forgotten
about the dragonfly candy treats
he had made several nights before.

When the treats were done
he had scooped them all up.
He put them in a large candy jar and
placed it on a high shelf.
Then proceeded to forget them.

While making the dragonflies,
Horace made a mistake.
Instead of adding a pinch of magic
he added a
WHOLE SCOOP.

One of the dragonfly candies was different than all the others.

This little dragonfly was full of magic and possibilities – and he was ready to leave the candy jar.

With a flap of his iridescent wings he flew to the top of the jar. With one push, POP went the lid. The little dragonfly swooped out into the candy shop in pure delight. Possibilities of what he could create ran through his tiny mind like a speeding train.

He saw possibilities everywhere.

With a twitch of his head
and a flap of his wings
he created
shiny candy bugles
that trumpeted magic
out into the air.

Magic that
one second before
had not been there.

Looking around he saw endless
yummy possibilities.

Peppermints, gumdrops, gingerbread cakes...

The little dragonfly swept his wings
out as far as he could reach.
He gave one blink.
He transformed it all into gumdrop cars
with peppermint wheels.
The cars zipped around the shop
and over gingerbread hills with icing frills.

He flew over a tray of
undecorated cupcakes.
He buzzed his beautiful wings.
Instantly elaborate icing and sprinkles
spread across each cupcake.

The cupcakes began dancing and twirling
to stack on a fancy plate.

On the dragonfly flew with more ideas
in his head. Magic fluttered out forming bars
of chocolate into a chocolate puppy covered
in shreds of coconut.
Bouncing balls and bones of candy
tumbled about in an acrobatic display.

Yipping and yapping, the puppy leaped
to the top of a candy tower.

Over pillars of jelly beans the dragonfly flew.
The beans scattered, bouncing here, there,
and everywhere.

Green, pink, purple, orange, brown, and yellow.

The jelly beans bounced to the rhythm
of the night magic.

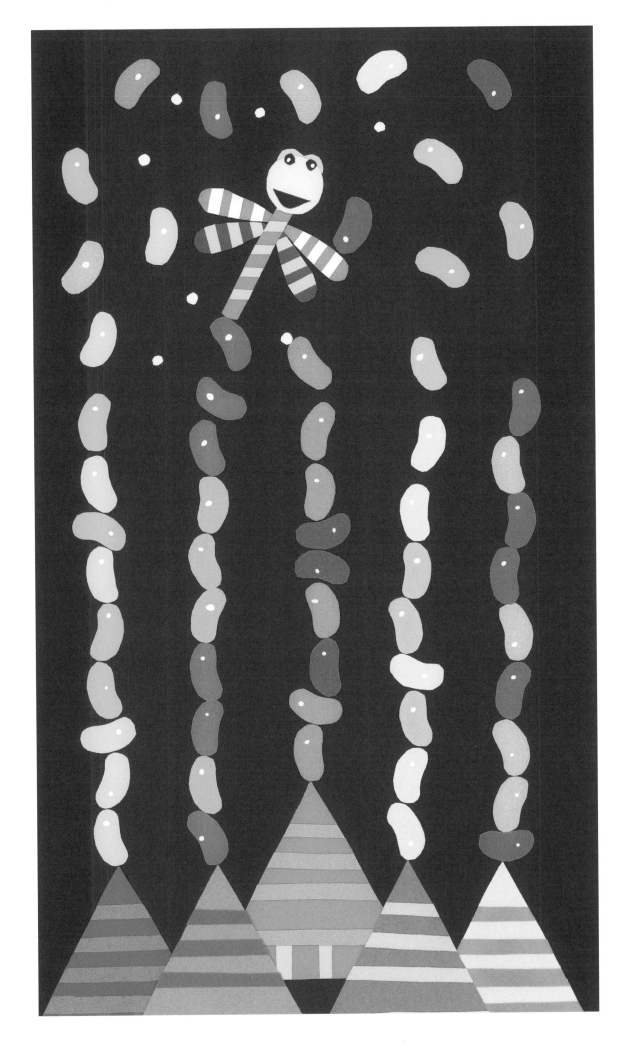

"OOOOH," the dragonfly thought
as he spotted a shelf of mugs.
"Wouldn't they be great
filled with hot chocolate?"

And hot chocolate swirled into the mugs
making clouds of chocolaty steam.

Marshmallows bounced to and fro
as if in a chocolaty dream.

Then, the dragonfly whirled 3 scoops
of ice cream into a tall glass.

Drizzling it all with fudgy gloopity gloop,
he added a cherry
right on the very top.

"I've done it!" the dragonfly exclaimed
while hovering in the air. He looked at
all the treats he had created. His job was done.
He had created something new from what
had been there all along.

He had wanted to show Horace that there
were always new possibilities, and he had.

With that, he flew up through the chimney
and into the night. He soared over the trees
to the hills beyond.

The little dragonfly had gone from the shop,
but his magic had not.

Horace Windemere awoke from his sound sleep. Something was different. He knew it was. What had awakened him? Had he heard a sound?

Horace quickly grabbed his robe and scurried down the stairs. His eyes popped open at what he saw.

Was he still dreaming? A magical display of sweet treats filled the counters and shelves.

A gumdrop car zoomed right over Horace's head.

Magic hung thick in the air.

How had this happened?

Who had made these wondrous treats?

Horace was so excited he punched
the air with his fist
and twirled in joyous glee.

He didn't know how it had happened.
But what he did know was that
all the possibilities he had not seen were
always right there.
Horace laughed to himself.
HOW had he not remembered?
Not remembered that
whenever a problem comes along
it is ALWAYS an opportunity
to discover new possibilities.

And from that day forward
that is exactly what he did.

Close your eyes tight,
let your mind fly,
dream all the possibilities
you've yet to try.

You are full of magic too.
You can create with all that you do.

ABOUT THE AUTHOR AND ILLUSTRATOR

Merrijo Wheaton lives in a small town in eastern Oregon with her partner, George Wheaton. The house they live in is close to the quaint downtown, which looks very much as it did 100 years ago when their home was built. An ancient clock tower, just over the trees and down the street, chimes out magical sounds on the hour.

In a studio filled with inspiration and lots of fun, Merrijo creates the illustrations for her whimsical stories by hand cutting and gluing every little piece of paper.

For the illustrations in her first book, ***THE BUG'S JOURNEY***, Merrijo was chosen as a finalist in the Next Generation Indie Book Awards competition.

Follow Merrijo on Instagram at aburdiousmjw, or on her web page, www.merrijowheaton.com.

A SPECIAL THANK YOU:

To George Wheaton -- who has been me through every step of this book, and hangs out in my studio sharing all the new enchantment.

To Marria Knight -- a kindred spirit who has given me her expertise and, most especially, her encouragement and support.

To Kathleen Ekbom - for her never ending enthusiasm and support.

To Palmetto Publishing -- for making the experience of publishing this book fun.

To you, the reader-- may you find the magic inside yourself.

If you feel so moved, please leave a review on Amazon or Goodreads.

Lightning Source UK Ltd.
Milton Keynes UK
UKHW021515171220
375249UK00003B/129